THREE DAYS ON A RIVER IN A RED CANOE

by Vera B. Williams

HOUGHTON MIFFLIN COMPANY

BOSTON

ATLANTA   DALLAS   GENEVA, ILLINOIS   PALO ALTO   PRINCETON

Thanks for rivers
and friends,
big and small

Acknowledgments

Grateful acknowledgment is made for permission to excerpt and/or reprint original or copyrighted materials, as follows:

Three Days on a River in a Red Canoe, by Vera B. Williams. Copyright © 1981 by Vera B. Williams. Reprinted by permission of Greenwillow Books, a division of William Morrow and Company, Inc.

Photography
31 (mr) Corbis-Bettmann **32-33** (bk) Jose Azel/AURORA
32 (l) Breck P. Kent/Animals Animals/Earth Scenes; (r) E.R. Degginger/Animals Animals/Earth Scenes **33** (l) (r) Zig Leszczynski/Animals Animals/Earth Scenes

2000 Impression

Houghton Mifflin Edition, 1997
Copyright © 1997 by Houghton Mifflin Company. All rights reserved.

Printed in the U.S.A.

ISBN: 0-395-81138-4

6789-B-02 01 00 99

I was the one who first noticed the red canoe for
sale in a yard on the way home from school.

My mom and my aunt Rosie and my cousin Sam
and I put our money together and bought it.
The people who sold it to us threw in two
paddles and two big old life jackets.

As soon as we got home with the canoe, Aunt Rosie and Mom took out their maps. The canoe trips they had taken before Sam or I was even born were marked in colors. They found a three-day trip that could be just right for us. Then we made lists of what we needed.
Then we went shopping.
Here are Sam and I in the store in new life jackets.
They cost a lot, but Aunt Rosie and Mom agreed we had to have them. And an extra paddle. And twenty feet of new rope. We also bought some packages of freeze-dried chicken and some dried apricots.

Here is everything we need for the trip. The food is packed tight in waterproof sacks. My cat Sixtoes is sitting on a sleeping bag. I wanted to take him, but Mom says a canoe is no place for a cat. I promised Sixtoes to bring him back a fish. Next to my shoes and Sam's shoes are new pocketknives. We never even noticed Aunt Rosie buying them for us in the store today.

4

WE DROVE AND DROVE AND DROVE AND DROVE AND DROVE AND DROVE AND DROVE AND DROVE AND DROVE AND DROVE

Here we are on our way early in the morning.

AND DROVE AND DROVE AND DROVE AND DROVE AND DROVE AND DROVE AND DROVE AND DROVE AND DROVE AND DROVE

WE DROVE AND DROVE

We drove all day. Now we are at the place Aunt Rosie and Mom had chosen for our first camp. We start on the river in the morning. Sam and I unloaded the car. Mom and Aunt Rosie put up the tent. We hurried to get inside before it got too dark and the mosquitoes took too many bites out of us. We lay in our tent listening to the river.

When I poked my head out in the morning,
everything was wet. Yet it wasn't even raining.
We couldn't see our car. We could hardly see the river.

We carried
our canoe
down to the
water anyway.

Here we are setting out for a small island it shows on the map.
We've packed all our things into the canoe. We are going
to fix our breakfast on the island when the sun
warms up the river and dries up the mist.

Here are Mom and Aunt Rosie paddling into a part of the river like a hot green tunnel. I fell asleep. I think Sam did too. It's good Mom and Rosie didn't. Right here is where they heard the roaring of the waterfall. But they had been listening for it. It was marked on their maps.

Here I am looking over the edge.

Aunt Rosie and Mom are lowering the canoe by ropes down over the waterfall. Sam and I climb up and down until we have carried all the gear to the bottom. We are going to camp here even though it's still early.

Here's our shower.

This is our kitchen. Aunt Rosie is the cook tonight.
We are going to try the crayfish we caught along
with our chicken and rice. For dessert Aunt Rosie
showed us how to cook fruit stew and dumplings.

This is the sink. You can stand right in it.
The rocks make all the shelves
and drainboards you need.
We use the sand as scouring powder.

Mom shows us some knots
we can use to tie up the canoe
and in putting up the tent.

12

TWO HALF HITCHES

1

PASS THE ROPE AROUND
A TREE OR STUMP

2

WITH YOUR LEFT HAND,
HOLD THE ROPE AT THE POINT
WHERE IT CROSSES OVER THE
LONGER PART OF THE ROPE

3

WITH YOUR RIGHT HAND,
REACH THROUGH THE LOOP
FOR THE SHORT END OF THE
ROPE. PULL THE END THROUGH
AND TIGHTEN THE LOOP

4

REPEAT 2 AND 3

FIRE

You don't need a bonfire to cook on.
Aunt Rosie made this kind of fire.
She kept it hot by adding small sticks.

DUMPLINGS

1 CUP DUMPLING-PANCAKE MIX (PAGE 6)
½ CUP OF WATER

Make a well in the mix. Pour in most
of the water. Mix quickly. Use only
enough water to make
a dough as thick as
soft ice cream.

Lumps don't matter. Push little spoonfuls
of dumpling onto the simmering fruit
as fast as you can. Cover. Cook until
the dumplings are just done but not hard
—about 10 minutes.

FRUIT STEW

3 HANDFULS OF DRIED APRICOTS (OR PEACHES)
HONEY OR SUGAR TO TASTE
ABOUT 3 CUPS OF WATER

Add enough water to the plastic bag to cover
the fruit. Do this when you
first make camp.

When you are ready to cook,
put the fruit, all the water, and the sweetening
in a pot.
Cover, and boil slowly.
Stir often.

Don't let the apricots burn. If water cooks
away, add more. This fruit stew
should be juicy. Cook till
apricots are soft—
about half an hour.

P.S. Don't burn your tongues.
We burned ours.

SAM AND I PUT UP
THE TENT BY OURSELVES

AUNT ROSIE TOLD ME
TO USE THE BACK
OF THE AXHEAD

SAM USED A ROCK

IT'S HARD TO GET THE PEGS IN
TIGHT SO THEY DON'T PULL OUT

YOU HAVE TO PULL
THE CORDS TIGHT TOO
SO THE TENT WON'T BE
LIKE AN OLD BALLOON

AND YOU HAVE TO TIE
A KIND OF KNOT
YOU CAN UNTIE EASILY

THIS IS AN EXTRA ROOF
CALLED A FLY

THE TENT CLOTH HAS TO LET IN AIR,
SO BY ITSELF IT CAN'T BE WATERPROOF

14

After supper we build up our fire and sit beside it. Mom tells us stories about the animals that like the nighttime. We watched the stars and the sparks of our fire going up to join them.

Sam isn't much of a weather predictor. But the rain didn't
bother us. We put up the tent so well hardly a drop of water
came through. In the morning we sat up in our sleeping bags
and ate crackers and raisins. Aunt Rosie made cocoa on the
little camping stove.

We set out on the river with all our
things even though it was pouring rain.
I am shaking my paddle at the sky
and yelling.

Suddenly as we came around this bend
in the river the sun came out through
a hole in the clouds. A big rainbow
spread across the sky.

SPOTTED SUNFISH BULLHEAD CATFISH REDFIN PICKEREL YELLOW PERCH

SCALE CARP BROOK TROUT BLACK CRAPPIE COMMON WHITE SUCKER

The rainbow faded away and fish started to jump all around us. We got the fishing lines baited and into the water. Sam caught the first fish. Then I caught one. Then Aunt Rosie caught two in a row. Afterward we spread out our things to dry on a sandy beach.

What Mom and Aunt Rosie like to do best is take the canoe through fast-moving water. They can follow all the curves of the current.
In the afternoon we canoe without stopping. Sam and I paddle too.

We came to a place where the river spread
out through a meadow. Grass grows right out of
the water and we canoed in the grass. It came up over
our heads and hid us. Aunt Rosie put her hand over my
mouth so I wouldn't frighten away the moose and her calf. But even
so, when they got wind of us, they ran right back into the woods.

When we discovered this island, we all agreed it was the place to
spend our third night. We plan to sleep right out under those trees.
The tent is up just in case of rain. The big dipper is out. The Milky
Way is spread right across the sky. There isn't one mosquito because
of the breeze.

That breeze turned into a wild wind in the middle of the night. Mom says it was almost hurricane strength. We caught the tent and the canoe just before the wind carried them off down the river. We did lose one pot and one cup. We spent the rest of the night curled up in the bushes. The branches creaked and whooshed all night long.

GREAT BLUE HERON

In the morning we can't believe this is the same river. It's so still.
Twigs and leaves and flowers float around us as we start our last
day on the river. We watch a muskrat swimming. A heron dives
for a fish. We feed crumbs to the ducks. Cows watch us having
a river visit.

WHISTLING
SWAN

MALLARD
DUCK

CANADA GOOSE

We canoe through a town. We come to a low stone bridge.
Sam gets excited. He stands up to wave. Mom yells,
"Sit down!" I reach over and pull him down.

Aunt Rosie and Mom brace hard on the other side. This keeps our canoe and everything in it from turning over.

But Sam ends up in the water. He swims to the rope Aunt Rosie throws out to him and we tow him to shore. Mom doesn't say much, but she looks upset. Aunt Rosie looks scared.
Sam changes to dry clothes and we canoe on.

Just past the train bridge Aunt Rosie asks Sam to stand up and see what's ahead. He gets up as though the canoe were a baby's cradle. He reports that the river is ending in a big lake. He says it looks like the edge of the world on the other side.

Aunt Rosie says that's because we're coming to the town dam. Mom points the canoe to cross the lake. There's no current and the wind is against us. I'm glad it's slow going.

When we get to the other side, our trip will be over.

And here we are... taking our canoe out onto the bank. Aunt Rosie showed me on the map where the river goes from here. She says it travels on through rocky places with lots of rapids. Someday, after lots of practice, we can go there.

But now we must catch a fish for my cat Sixtoes. And Aunt
Rosie is going to talk with other campers and find a lift back
to our car Ladybug so we can get home tonight. Mom says
canoeing back up the river against the current would be very,
very hard even if we had time.

Way past midnight we turn into our own street. One
by one we stumble into the house. I go to sleep to the
sound of Sixtoes chewing on his fish. It seems I can
still hear the sound of the river running over the rocks.

THREE DAYS ON A RIVER IN A RED CANOE

CONTENTS:

River Wildlife

Who else lives along a river besides people?

The Life Cycle of a River

Find out how rivers are formed.

Level 3
Theme 3: Environment

River Wildlife

Many different animals live in and along our rivers. Freshwater fish live upstream and down. Reptiles, such as turtles, and crustaceans, such as crayfish, live in the shallow water along a river's banks. Birds make their nests nearby. These animals rely on each other for food and on river plants for protection.

Trout are strong swimmers. They live in rivers and streams where the water is cold and fast moving. This is a young brook trout. A brook trout's spots are usually pink or cream in color. Mature trout eat other fish and crayfish.

Crayfish, also called crawfish, live in rivers and along lake shores. They eat snails, small fish, and young insects. They are usually smaller than six inches in length and can be various colors. This is a blue crayfish.

This **turtle** is a northern diamondback terrapin. They live in freshwater and along salt marshes. They eat crabs, clams, and green plants. Female terrapins, which are larger than males, can grow as large as nine inches.

Herons are birds that have pointed bills and long thin necks. They nest in bushes and trees, but wade along the shores of rivers and lakes to fish for food. The great blue heron, shown above, is the largest heron in North America.

Life Cycle of a River

A river begins as a stream of water, created by rain and melting snow high in the mountains. Streams join together as they flow downhill to create a powerful river. The river slows down on flat land, becoming deeper and wider. Often a river curves back and forth or splits off to form other bodies of water. By the time the river reaches the sea, its water moves slowly. Water from the sea, rivers, and lakes turns to water vapor and is released into the air, forming clouds. Wind blows this water vapor higher, and soon the vapor turns to rain or snow and falls again on the mountains.

7 Wind Wind blows water vapor higher, forming clouds.

wind

Water vapor is also released by plant life.

6 Evaporation Sea water changes to water vapor.

5 Mouth The river runs into the sea.

river

sea

1 **Precipitation** Water vapor changes to rain, snow, sleet, or hail and falls on high ground.

2 **Source** Streams of water begin to run down the mountain.

mountain

3 **Stream** Small streams combine to form a deep, wide river.

Lake water changes to water vapor.

lake

4 **Meandering** The river water slows and follows a winding course. The river splits to form a smaller river and a lake.

Water seeps underground and flows to the sea.